ZOMBIE SEAGULLS

ZOMBIE SEAGULLS

and 13 other bite-sized nightmares!

JIM BOLONE

M · P · P
www.MissionPointPress.com

 Mission Point Press

Published by Mission Point Press
MissionPointPress.com

ISBN: 978-1-968761-25-7
LoC Control Number: 2026909920

Printed in the United States of America

Dedication

For my students, points of light each one, who taught me more than I could ever quantify, like trying to count all those stars in the sky.

Acknowledgments

Thanks to the publishing team at Mission Point Press, including Jen Wahi, Jackie Barnes, Hart Cauchy, Michelle DiMercurio, and Aimé Merizon. Thanks also to Anna Bolone, Rusty Young, and Quinn Staten for the beta reads and suggestions.

CONTENTS

Preface   IX

Fly with Me   1
Chuckles   15
The Jar Witch   21
Gargoyle of the West Bluff   31
I Scream   43
Come to Bed, Mommy   49
Aunt Ginny's Undead   57
Voices Calling at British Landing   63
Storm Maiden   69
Zombie Seagulls   75
Skull Cave   87
Pieces of Madame   93
Bullseye   107
Wendigo   115

About the Author   125

PREFACE

SCARY stories have always been my guilty pleasure. As a kid I was hooked on old television shows like *The Twilight Zone*, *Night Gallery*, and *Tales from the Crypt*, watching wide-eyed and sometimes through my fingers, regretting every second at bedtime. These weren't simple scary tales; they were master classes in suspense and emotion, often ending with a chilling twist.

As a teacher, I've discovered something crucial about reading: It's essential, yes, but it's not always easy to get reluctant readers hooked. The problem isn't the students or the schools—sometimes it's the stories. To truly captivate, a story has to be sharp, fast, and clear. Not every narrative needs to sprawl across hundreds of pages; sometimes, a quick, bite-sized nightmare is exactly what a reader needs.

Whether you're a seasoned horror fan or stepping into the shadows for the first time, I invite you to read at your own risk. These fourteen stories are short and powerful, designed to grip, and maybe haunt, you.

Oh—and you might want to sleep with a light on.

FLY WITH ME

ITS hull slicing through the water, the ferry rounded the chunky limestone breakwall. It slowed, executed a tight U-turn, and bobbed gently against the dock.

It was noon on Mackinac Island. Distant hoofbeats clopped on Main Street and a tinny version of "Reveille" (the traditional military bugle call used to wake soldiers) blared from a loudspeaker at Fort Mackinac.

Tim cautiously stepped off the boat first, greeted by a gull that screamed overhead before vanishing into the rising fog. Aiden followed, eyes scanning the dock. Nolan brought up the rear, smiling his usual big, dumb grin. They'd finally arrived at Fort Mackinac. A reward for earning Honor Scout status—a week of history lessons, chores, and service at the fort.

The boys looked at each other and held their noses.

"Manure," Nolan muttered. "Smells like my grandparents' farm in Ohio."

"You mean horse crap," Aiden said, lowering his hand. "We better get used to it. Breathe through your mouth."

Nolan followed suit. "Agreed."

Tim's hand fanned the front of his face. "But if I breathe through my mouth, I'm inhaling horse crap."

"Suit yourself," Aiden shrugged.

Tim scoffed, breathed deep, and exhaled.

The barracks sat on a rise surrounded by tall dune grass. Inside, a crooked crucifix hung above the bedroom door, twisted at the nail. Metal-framed beds groaned and squeaked as the boys placed their belongings on musty mattresses. Varnished knotty pine walls reflected faint sunlight.

Tim went into the bathroom. "Hey, what the—there's no lights in here," his voice echoed.

"Think they did that on purpose?" Aiden asked.

No one answered.

Lunch was canned soup and bread gone hard with age. Scouts chatted over trays. A kid named Harris claimed he'd heard screeching in the attic—bats, maybe. He said the island had caves—deep ones—and people fell in and didn't come back.

Aiden rolled his eyes. "Just stories."

"I read somewhere that bats do scream in their sleep," Nolan said, staring out the mess hall window.

Tim didn't laugh. He remembered the seagull that flew past them on the dock. The sound of its cry. Unlike a gull.

After lunch the scouts worked on skills, then hiked along some of the horse trails in the woods. The sky overhead was clear and blue; the troop walked single file along a narrow path flanked by thick woods, their scoutmaster paced alongside. Nolan, Tim, and Aiden lagged behind.

"This island is cool," Nolan said. He turned and, walking backward, looked at

Tim and Aiden with a smirk. "Tonight. Us. We gotta sneak back up here."

Tim looked surprised. "For what?"

Aiden and Nolan smiled at each other. Nolan tapped Tim's arm. "Seriously? We're on Mackinac Island. Let's live a little."

Tim shook his head. "And get sent back home after only one day here?"

"Not going to happen," Aiden said. "It's an island and I don't think they're gonna send us anywhere."

Tim scoffed.

The scoutmaster called from the front. "Let's get a move on you three."

Tim was the first to scurry up.

Dinner came, as did clean up. Campfire was at 8:00 p.m. The scouts sang a few songs, told a few stories, and ate a few snacks before heading back to the barracks for lights out at 9:30.

Beneath a cloud-masked moon, the three boys ran behind the fort, past the stone wall, and up into the wooded hills. Only the crickets and wind accompanied the crunch of their footsteps. Flashlights in hand, they walked past the horse trail they'd hiked with the troop earlier in the day and took another a little farther up. A few minutes into their journey, they stumbled upon it.

A cave.

Aiden's flashlight beam caught it behind a veil of wild ivy—a hole in the rock like an enormous, yawning mouth exhaling cold air.

Tim clicked his tongue, shook his head, and peered through the vines. "Not sure about going in there. Who knows what's inside."

"That's exactly why we should check it out," Aiden grinned.

Together, they crouched and entered. The dampness and mold were pungent. The walls were craggy and wet. Faint drawings covered them—burnt-looking symbols, some with wings or eyes, others like human figures drawn upside down with stitched-shut mouths.

Tim touched one and his finger came off wet. "These people, look at their mouths."

The fort's barracks' bell rang in the distance. Six gongs. An unexpected rush of flapping wings erupted above them.

Bats.

They weren't flying; they were falling. Like rotten fruit.

One struck Nolan's shoulder, crawled some, then bit deep. He slapped it away, grimacing. As the other boys looked on in horror, Nolan shook his head and breathed heavy. "I'm fine," he said, rubbing his shoulder.

Aiden motioned with his thumb. "Let's go."

Tim nodded. "To the nurse."

Nolan walked in front, his hand still on his shoulder.

That night, wind pushed hard against the barracks.

Tim woke to a sound. Scratching.

Nolan stood at the window. "They're flying now," he said, his warped reflection staring back at him. "It's the bell. It calls them." He didn't blink. His breath fogged the glass, and with one finger, he drew wings.

Tim frowned. The camp nurse had brushed off the bite. "Bats carry disease, not venom," she'd said. Tim didn't believe her and wasn't convinced all she could do for Nolan was pour peroxide over the bite, slap a bandage on it, and give him a mint.

The next day, Nolan didn't eat. His skin paled. He smiled less, slept more. He stopped hanging with Tim and Aiden. One morning, he refused to go outside. "Too bright," he muttered. Just before bedtime Aiden caught him shirtless in the bathroom, staring into a mirror, mumbling. His chest bore several long, bleeding scratches. Nolan cupped water, splashed his chest, pressed a towel to the wounds, and walked past Aiden without a word.

Later, at the scout campfire, the troop was enjoying s'mores, except Nolan, who'd been quietly staring at the fire with a half-smile. He turned and made eye contact with Tim, and then to Tim's shock, Nolan snagged a moth near the flame and placed it in his mouth and chewed. Disgusted, Tim looked around to see if anyone, especially Aiden, had seen what Nolan had done. No one did.

Tim and Aiden had not forgotten the strange symbols in the cave, and after extinguishing the campfire, they searched the scout chapel for answers. In a back room, they found an old book: *Landmarks and Lore of the Straits.* Its spine was cracked; its pages smelled of smoke. One map showed Eagle Point. A red X marked the cave. Below it, a scrawled note read: *Sacred ground. Do not disturb. The old ones do not sleep.* Further on, a torn page hid a dry, pressed wing. At the bottom: *One is chosen; the others feed.* Tim closed the book. He and Aiden locked eyes in horror.

That night, Tim whispered, "Did you see Nolan at the campfire?"

Aiden nodded. "Barely said a word."

"Maybe because he was eating bugs."

"What?"

"I saw him catch a moth. Bare-handed. Snagged it in mid-air. Popped it in his mouth and chewed like candy."

"No one else saw?"

"Nobody. He looked at me like he didn't even care."

Aiden half smiled and looked up at the ceiling. "Let's see. So we had s'mores and Nolan had a s'moth."

They both laughed quietly, but not for long. What Nolan had done wasn't normal, and they knew it. Aiden had trouble sleeping that night. He couldn't stop thinking about something he'd seen at the campfire—something he hadn't told Tim. "Nolan doesn't make a shadow anymore," he muttered to himself.

Later, Nolan climbed from bed and stood over another scout. Silent. Watching him.

When the boy stirred, Nolan smiled. His teeth were too long, too sharp. At breakfast, Tim spotted Nolan chewing something. Small, insectoid legs stuck out of his lips. Still twitching. Aiden saw it too. Well after bedtime, Nolan began talking in his sleep. Strange mutterings bubbled out of his mouth in an alien tongue.

Neither boy could sleep anymore. Quietly gathering up their clothes and a flashlight, they headed outside, the old door creaking shut behind them.

They returned to the cave. This time without Nolan, and this time there were no birds chirping or wind in the trees.

Inside, it was colder than before. The cave had changed. They found a new tunnel and crawled through to a chamber where bones littered the floor—some small and others too large for comfort. One skull—a deer?—was marked with tight, jagged bite marks. On the wall was a carving they hadn't seen before. It was a man, upside down with bat wings erupting and rising from his back. It had Nolan's face.

Both boys returned to the barracks. Usually they were brave, or at least pretended to be. But on the quiet walk back, surrounded by darkness, they were scared beyond words.

Then came the storm. The wind screamed, windows slammed, thunder pounded like boots overhead. When it passed, a scoutmaster entered the barracks, making sure everyone was alright. Nolan was gone. The scoutmaster, worried, asked them to check the mess hall.

They agreed. But they both knew where Nolan had really gone.

Darkness fell in the woods, and as they walked, they noticed something strange on the forest floor. Something *crunchy*. Looking down, they saw feathers and bones.

A trail of claw marks led to the cave. It was wider than before. Inside, the air pulsed like breath.

In the back chamber, they found him,

hanging from the ceiling by his feet. Nolan's eyes opened. They were oddly shaped. "Fly with me," he said. His voice was wind. The bell rang. Not from the fort—from the cave itself. One time, two times, then three.

Stone cracked. The walls moved. Things stepped out. Tall, their skin like dried mud, and wings thin as parchment, faces with scowls, arms too long, eyes black. Their teeth curved backward. They stank like sun-baked roadkill.

Aiden shrieked.

One lunged. Nolan dropped—no longer human. His mouth a row of needles. He shrieked like a bat and charged.

Tim shined his flashlight at the nearest creature.

It screamed, smoked, then melted in a gurgly slop smelling of bile.

"They burn in light!" Tim shouted.

They ran. Branches grabbed and tore at them. Behind them, they heard flapping. Aiden stumbled as a claw caught his back. Tim dragged him upright. They barely reached the chapel and threw open the doors. The bell hung in the steeple like a corpse. Tim rang it again and again. The stained glass pulsed. The creatures stopped at the door, hissed, and fled. Nolan looked back once, turned, and flew away.

By morning, Nolan's bunk was made. His name was gone from the roster. His toothbrush was still there. The bristles were bloody.

Aiden stopped speaking and slept with his flashlight on.

Tim found him in the chapel one night, staring up at the bell, unresponsive.

Tim, not sure how to help his friend, took the book from the chapel and fled. He burned it in the mess hall stove. Page by page. Until the final page, as it curled and burned, revealed a line Tim managed to see:

When one is marked, the island keeps them. The caves will call again.

Late on their final night, long after lights out, the chapel bell rang.

No rope pulled. No wind blew. Just one sound, loud, low, final.

Tim closed his eyes and fell asleep. Not long after, Aiden did too.

Somewhere, not very far away, Nolan hesitated. He bowed his head in brief remembrance, looked up and screeched, then spread his wings and soared into the night sky.

CHUCKLES

Every summer, Ruby's parents dragged her to Mackinac Island like it was some kind of reward. On the island there were no cars. In fact, no motor vehicles were allowed at all. What made things even worse was having no Wi-Fi and, most of all, Ruby's younger cousin, Max.

This summer, if Ruby wasn't going to be riding her scooter or texting friends, she'd at least have fun irritating Max.

Max was the kind of kid who always had to prove how "not scared" of things he was. If a sign read Do Not Enter, Max would be the one to go—twice. So when Ruby told him the legend of Robinson's Folly, he laughed. "They called it a 'folly' because some guy fell off a cliff?" he asked, skipping a rock toward the edge. "I don't care. I like it here, clown or no clown."

"No," Ruby said. "It's because they built the stage too close to the edge. People used to perform there. That's when Chuckles came."

She didn't need to explain. Every generation on the island had heard the story of Chuckles the Clown.

Ruby continued. "They said he came to the first summer fair in 1883, big shoes and all, heavy white makeup, and a permanent smile that looked like someone carved it with a knife. Chuckles never really spoke. His words spilled out as a strange kind of laughter.

"One night, a little boy went missing. Eyewitnesses claimed there was a clown that had been following the boy. They blamed Chuckles. All the townspeople went after him, chasing him to Robinson's Folly. He ran as fast as he could without any concern about the cliff. Some say he tripped on one of his own clown shoes. Others say people in the crowd pushed him. But the last anyone saw was that white-painted face, tumbling through the air, laughing all the way down, with only a single tattered and dusty clown shoe left at the Folly."

Max rolled his eyes. "You really believe that?"

Ruby didn't answer. A sudden gust of wind tousled her hair.

Max tripped. His foot had caught on something half-buried in the dirt—a mask. Not a plastic one for kids, but one made of porcelain, cracked and stained with age and soil. It was an eerily grotesque clown face, the mouth pulled wide in an exaggerated grin. "Cool," Max said.

Ruby felt sick. "Don't touch it, Max," she snapped.

But it was already in his hands, and he wiped it off with his fingers.

Late that night, Ruby heard something. Laughter, dark and off-key, like it knew a wicked secret. She bolted upright and glanced at Max's bed. He wasn't there. She got up and quietly searched, calling his name in a concerned tone. She found him on the hotel porch, staring toward the bluff.

"I saw him," Max said, his face without expression.

"Who?"

His voice trembled, but his lips curled up slightly, like he couldn't stop himself from smiling. "The clown . . . Chuckles."

The fair opened the next day. Women wore Victorian dresses. Lemon ice was served. A barbershop quartet sang out of tune. But Ruby couldn't enjoy any of it. Something was wrong. People seemed too happy. Their laughter dragged on for too long. Then the first child disappeared. Charlie, a six-year-old boy, was last seen near the puppet stage. A few days later it was a girl. And then another. Ruby tried to tell the adults, but they dismissed her.

"It's just a game," one of them said. "The kids will show up."

But they didn't.

Ruby had a plan. She and Max went back to the cliff that night, the clown mask stuffed in her backpack. "We give it back," she said. "Whatever we woke up, maybe it just wants to finish the show."

Max didn't respond. His face was pale. His smile—still stuck there—twitched.

They reached the edge. The wind howled and waves crashed below. And then came the fog.

Chuckles stepped out from the mist, wearing only one clown shoe. His ruffled collar was stained red. His gloves were shredded. But the mask, Ruby realized, wasn't a mask at all. It was his face, and it didn't move. His black marble eyes looked *through* her and liked what it saw. The air around him writhed, the way heat does above fire. His hand was long, his fingers jerking like a marionette, and that sinister laugh flooded out.

Max screamed and fell to his knees, his hands over his ears.

Ruby pulled out the mask. "Take it!" she shouted, flinging it into the air.

Chuckles caught it midair, one impossibly long arm whipping out like a rubber band. Then he bowed. With one hand, he touched Max's head. The smile faded. Max sobbed. Chuckles turned, mask in hand, and walked backward into the mist, bowing again and again, even as the fog inhaled him.

In the morning, the missing children returned, confused, but safe. They said they'd been watching a show. A funny man with a funny face. He made them laugh until it hurt. Little Charlie had blood under his fingernails but no memory of why.

No one believed them, except for Ruby and Max.

Now, every summer, Ruby leaves a single daisy at the edge of Robinson's Folly. A thank-you. A warning. Max doesn't talk about it, but he always goes with her.

On this particular afternoon, Ruby looked at Max's face and shuddered. When the sun shone just right, she thought she saw a faint red line across his mouth.

THE JAR WITCH

"HEY guys, let's go swimming, then maybe get ice cream at the Cannonball," Johnny Zindel pulled his shirt over his head like the decision was final.

Jordan Riggi and Mason Rudolph nodded.

"I'm down," Jordan said. "It's brutal out."

Sammy Toliver hesitated. "I think I'm gonna ride instead. Maybe take the horse trail through the woods. It's cooler in the shade."

Johnny raised an eyebrow. "Seriously? You're skipping swimming and ice cream for the woods and mosquitoes?"

Sammy shrugged. "Just not feeling the water today. I haven't had any 'me time' in a while."

Mason's grandmother sat on the porch,

her knitting needles clicking rhythmically. She glanced up, eyes sharp beneath heavy brows. "You boys heading into the woods?" she asked.

"Just Sammy," Mason said, nodding toward his friend. "Going full hermit."

The old woman lowered her knitting. "Stay on the path," she warned. "And if you see flashing glass or bones hanging from the trees, turn back. That forest holds things older than this island."

The boys exchanged uneasy looks. "Here we go," Johnny muttered under his breath.

She ignored him and spoke while knitting. "There was a woman once. Morganna. Said she was a healer, but the village feared her. They burned her house, chased her into the woods. She swore she'd never leave." She stopped knitting and looked at the boys. "They called her a witch, but they went to her when their babies burned with fever. Then they turned on her. They believed she stole what she cured."

Mason gave a half-laugh. "So what, she haunts it now?"

"She doesn't haunt," his grandmother said. "She keeps."

The boys fell silent.

"She traps souls in jars, glass jars filled with dark liquid. You'll see them if you go too far. Hanging from the ceiling, dozens. Maybe hundreds. People she's claimed."

A breeze stirred through the trees, sending a chill down Sammy's spine.

Jordan broke the silence. "Okay, I'm getting in the lake before I turn into soup."

"Yeah, let's bounce," Johnny said, already walking off.

Mason nodded at his grandmother. "We'll be back before dinner." They headed for the beach, laughing, towels slung over shoulders.

Sammy lingered behind awhile. "Jars, huh?" he asked, half-joking.

The old woman fixed him with a steady gaze. "Once she sees you . . . there's no hiding. They say she keeps them out of vengeance."

"Well, I'm riding anyway." Sammy gave a tight nod and pushed off on his bike.

The tires crunched gravel, then dirt as he entered the trail. Behind him, laughter faded. The trees closed in.

The trail narrowed almost immediately after the fork. Sammy stood on his pedals, weaving around ruts and patches of soft earth. The air smelled of pine and hot soil. Here, deep in the island's interior, there were no tourists, no carriages, only the quiet roll of tires and the rhythmic scraping of the chain guard.

He pushed harder, until something sharp flashed to his left, a peel of sunlight bouncing off a jagged shard swinging from a tree. He braked hard, skidding slightly in the dirt. A frayed string hung from a crooked branch, a piece of broken glass dangled at the end, catching light like a warning.

Sammy dismounted and pushed through a curtain of weeping willow vines that snagged his shirt a little, but he ducked low and continued on. The farther in he went, the colder it grew, unnaturally cold, like walking into a freezer. Then he saw it.

An old, crooked sun-beaten hut stood in a clearing, half-swallowed by vines, its roof sagging beneath decades of moss. Bones, small ones like from birds and rabbits, hung from the eaves by fraying strings. Some of them were bleached white, others still flecked with fur. His breath caught. He should have left, but he didn't. The door was half-open, crooked on its hinges while shadow flickered inside. "Hello?" he asked, his voice cracking as he walked closer.

The door creaked wider. The hanging bones swayed. It was dim inside, the only light a candle burning without a wick, its flame steady and blue. The walls were lined with jars. Dozens of them. Each filled with murky liquid and something faintly pulsing inside, something alive. Then, a sound. A tapping, from *inside* one of the jars. Sammy jumped back. Rasping laughter spilled from the rafters above. He looked up. A figure hovered in the corner. She had long red hair, wild and knotted with leaves. Where her eyes should be, smooth skin stretched tight over empty sockets, thin veins writhing beneath. She opened her mouth and a weird sound seeped from her lips and slithered into his ears.

The door banged shut.

Sammy ran to it, clawing at a handle that was gone. Behind him, the jars shivered.

One rocked forward and fell but didn't

break. It rolled across the floor and stopped at his feet. Inside, a face stared back at him. It was his own. His reflection twisted, his mouth opening in a silent scream, hands pressed against the glass. The witch spoke again.

Everything went dark.

The next afternoon, Jordan, Johnny, and Mason walked the trail near the woods, calling Sammy's name.

Jordan stopped and held his finger near his lips. "What was that?"

Johnny squinted toward the trees. A glass shard swung slowly from a string tied to a crooked stick. Then, a sound. *Tap. Tap.* Faint, like it came from underground or from inside something.

They all heard it.

"Mason? Johnny? Guys . . . please . . . help . . ."

It came from deep within the woods. They couldn't find where the voice had come from, and after calling out, the only response was the soft wind and the distant clinking of glass.

The next day, the boys asked around,

but no one had seen Sammy. His bike was gone. His phone went straight to voicemail. His parents thought he'd gone out with the other boys again, until Johnny, Jordan, and Mason told them otherwise.

By late afternoon, locals were combing the woods near the horse trail: volunteers, a deputy, and Mason's dad. But the forest was big, tangled, and old. Paths crisscrossed like veins, most of them leading to dead ends.

The boys stayed behind, pacing the edge of the woods, guilty, silent, sunburned, dry-throated. Jordan saw it again: the glint, the glass shard twisting, illuminated in the sunlight. "This is where we saw it," he breathed.

Johnny pushed forward, parting underbrush. "Sammy! If this is a joke, it's not funny!"

No answer. Only silence.

They stepped deeper into the woods, past trees with bark like wrinkled skin, the air thick with humid heat and silence. Until Mason froze. "Oh God."

There it was, the crooked hut.

Johnny picked up a heavy branch. "If this turns into some Blair Witch crap, I'm out."

As if in response, the door creaked open by itself.

Jordan swallowed. "Yo, I hate this. The place smells like death and gym socks."

"But we can't just leave," Mason said. "What if Sammy's in there?" They all nodded their heads in agreement and entered the hut.

Inside, jars lined every wall. Shelves sagged under the weight of them, filled with murky fluid and twitching shapes.

Mason backed up, hand over his mouth. "This can't be real."

Johnny's eyes locked on one jar sitting on a wooden stool, lit by a strange greenish glow. "Guys . . ."

Jordan moved in beside him, slower now. "No way. That's . . . dude, that's Sammy."

The boy in the jar stared out at them, eyes wide. His mouth moved soundlessly, but they all knew what he said: *Help me.*

Jordan reached out, fingers trembling. "Sammy? Bro, what the—"

The temperature dropped ten degrees. Something stirred from above.

Mason's breath hitched. "Run!" he yelled.

They did. They didn't stop, not until they hit sunlight.

The boys returned with adults, but the hut was gone, vanished without a trace. After a week of searching, almost everyone had given up, and tourists once again walked the trails.

Sammy's parents hung flyers, offered rewards. But no one found anything. Except one.

Mason had hardly ever been in his grandma's bedroom, but when the wind blew through her window and slammed her door closed, he thought he'd do her a favor and close the window. On his way out he stopped, and the skin on the back of his neck tingled at what he saw. Over his grandma's headboard was a large glass fragment hanging from an old string.

GARGOYLE OF THE WEST BLUFF

THE Callahans came to Mackinac Island to rebuild their lives.

Paul Callahan called it "a fresh start." His wife, Erin, called it "an adventure."

Their fifteen-year-old daughter, Samantha, called it a mistake.

Twelve-year-old Danny mostly called it boring.

Until the statue.

The house, a crumbling Victorian on the West Bluff, loomed with dark windows and iron fretwork, its towers standing like sleeping sentinels. Its floorboards creaked even when no one walked through it. The wind moved through the halls like it was searching for something.

They found the statue on their second day.

It stood in the center of the overgrown backyard, half-swallowed by brambles, decayed leaves, and apple trees choked with vines. The gargoyle was the size of a man, crouched low on a weather-pounded pedestal. Its wings curled inward, tightly, like a scorpion's tail, claws curled as if ready to strike, its head tilted slightly forward. Its eyes were thin, set in deep hollows. One fang chipped. The gargoyle's stone skin, split with spiderweb cracks, was slick with morning dew. Beneath the moss, it was . . . darker.

"Creepy," Samantha said.

Paul chuckled. "It's art. Real Gothic stuff. They used to put these things on cathedrals to ward off evil."

Danny spit out his chewing gum. "I think it's evil."

"It's just a statue," Paul said, slapping the statue's back. The slap gave off a strange, hollow thud, like something inside had stirred.

Erin winced and backed up. "I wouldn't do that, Paul. It's probably full of spiders."

Samantha stared at it a moment longer, unease prickling under her skin.

Later in the night, she woke to scratching. Not from her room, from outside. She pulled back the curtain and looked out. There it was, still in the yard. But the shadow it cast on the lawn stretched too far. It didn't match with the moonlight, and it was facing the wrong direction. And to make things weirder, the shadow moved, barely, but just enough to notice.

She blinked, stared, then gasped.

She didn't sleep very well, if at all. In the morning, she told Danny.

"You had a nightmare," he said.

"No I didn't. I was awake. Like, for the entire night. The shadow moved."

Danny was already walking off. "You're always seeing stupid stuff."

"You know I'm not making this up, Danny."

He shrugged, then paused. "Fine. Let's prove it then." He rigged his motion-activated camera outside her window, facing the yard. It blinked green. "We'll catch the son of a gun."

They didn't. Not the first night, or the second.

Each morning, the footage was gone—blank, corrupted, or eerily silent with flashes of static. Once, it recorded only twenty-nine minutes of white noise.

The third night, the gargoyle's claw retracted. Samantha swore it hadn't been before. And the next, its head was lifted. Then, they found the bird, a half-eaten robin laid at the base of the statue. Its wings were missing, the eyes picked clean. No footprints. No blood trail.

Max, their golden retriever, sniffed once, whined, and backed away, tail tucked. He refused to step into the yard again.

"Something is wrong," Samantha said.

Danny locked his window.

Things escalated with the full moon. The light was silver and sharp. The island was still.

Samantha still couldn't sleep. She paced, restless, drawn again to the window. She saw the deer first, grazing and peaceful. Then the statue, gone. Her mouth opened to scream, but no sound came out.

From the trees, the gargoyle emerged, moving with sickening fluidity. Its wings spread, massive and unnervingly thin, as if stitched from flesh and stone. It dropped from a branch without sound, landing inches from the deer.

Then it fed. Samantha watched, frozen, fighting a gag reflex as it tore through the deer with feral urgency, teeth clacking, claws splitting hide and bone. Its tongue—wet and black—flicked around the blood. Its eyes glowed faintly gold, and as it ate, it let out a sound that was almost human, a low moan that grew into a growl. Before dawn, it limped back to the pedestal.

By sunrise, it was stone again.

Danny didn't believe Samantha. "You dreamed it."

"Look at me," she said. Her voice shook. "I was awake all night."

He tried to laugh it off. But he wasn't laughing for long.

A couple nights later, he'd gone to reset the motion sensor, grumbling about battery drain. Samantha begged him not to go. Ten minutes later, he ran back, breathless, pale as clay.

"Something was out there," he panted. "Something . . . not right."

He'd heard wings. Not flapping, but gliding. A massive shape passed over him; he felt its hot breath on his neck followed by hiss like boiling oil. His mind went blank. He ran for his life.

"It chased me, Sam," he said, gasping for breath. "It wanted me."

They told their parents.

Paul exploded. "Are you both trying to sabotage this vacation?"

Erin looked tired. "You've always had vivid imaginations, but this? This is too much."

"Dad," Danny said softly. "What if it's real?"

Paul placed his hands on his head. "Enough. Enough!"

Rain fell from a night sky and pattered on the roof as a thunderstorm slowly rolled over the island.

The next morning, Paul and Erin were gone. The bed was made. Their phones left on the dresser. No note. No text. No good-bye. Max whimpered from under the couch, his ears flat. Samantha and Danny searched room after room, from the attic to the basement. Nothing.

Finally, they ventured into the backyard. Samantha screamed.

Paul's shoe—ripped, soaked in black slime—sat near the gargoyle's pedestal. Bits of dirt clung to it, and something moved inside, writhing.

Danny found the cloth next, a scrap of their mother's blouse, blood-stained and caught in the thorns behind the statue. He picked it up slowly. "Mom . . . ?" Thunder rumbled again. The wind whirled overhead.

Samantha looked up and felt her knees go weak. The gargoyle was gone.

Not on the pedestal.

Not in the yard.

Shortly after sunset something landed on the roof with a *THUD*. They ran inside, locking every door they passed.

Samantha pulled Danny into the pantry. They heard something dragging across the roof, slow and deliberate. Like talons scraping shingles. After waiting for what seemed like hours in tense silence, they peeked outside. Through a crack in the curtains, they saw something deep in the trees. Not the gargoyle. Something taller. It stepped forward, glowing eyes, long limbs, too many joints. It crackled like burnt bone.

Danny whispered, "That's what it's been fighting."

"What?"

"It wasn't hunting us, Sam. It's been protecting us. From that."

Outside, they heard an inhuman scream, crazed and disjointed.

The gargoyle leapt from the roof, crashing into the shadow-thing. Fire sparked from the impact, sound splitting the air like a thunderclap. Samantha saw it through the window, just for a second.

With ferocious abandon, it tore at the thing's throat, stone teeth shredding smoke-flesh, wings battered and burning. The monster howled and vanished, not dying, but retreating into the dark woods.

The sun returned the next morning. Their parents didn't.

The gargoyle was back on its pedestal, cracked and bleeding sap-thick black fluid from one eye. Its claw now extended outward, palm up. Samantha placed her hand in it. The stone was warm.

Now, at night, they sleep lightly. They hear the breathing sometimes, deep in the trees. And once in a while, they hear footsteps on the roof. But they don't run anymore. Because now they understand. The gargoyle is not the monster.

It's the only thing keeping something worse from getting in.

No one ever came looking for Paul and Erin Callahan. No search party. No police. Not even a ranger.

The kids tried calling. The phones worked, the lines connected. But when they spoke, the people on the other end couldn't hear them. Or something interfered.

They went to the docks, hoping to escape on a ferry. It never came.

Danny stood at the docks one afternoon, eyes on the gray lake. He waited six hours. No boat. No sound. Just fog rolling across the open water.

It was as if the island had drifted a little farther from the world.

Like it was being cut loose. They didn't try to leave after that. The forest made it clear they weren't supposed to.

Twice they tried hiking across the island to reach the fort. Both times, the trees shifted, paths looping back to where they started. The shadows under the canopy grew unnaturally thick, like the air itself was bruised. On the second attempt, Danny stepped off the trail and nearly fell into a sinkhole, wide and wet, full of bones and vines. Some of the bones were human. They didn't try a third time.

Final entry from Samantha's journal:

I think we were wrong about everything. The gargoyle wasn't here to protect us. It was here to guard the gate. To keep something locked inside the earth. Something buried when the island was still young. But now it's waking up.

The statue's gone. The trees move even when there's no wind. Danny hasn't spoken in a day. His eyes are cloudy. He keeps humming a song I've never heard over and over.

I think I saw Mom outside last night.

She was floating.

Whatever is coming, I don't think we're going to survive it. But I don't think we were ever meant to. I can only hope.

The pedestal is empty again. And the moon is full.

I SCREAM

THE line outside McNally's Fudge Shop stretched down Main Street, past the gift stores and bike rentals, all the way to the docks.

Tourists shuffled forward like cattle, glistening foreheads, shirts damp with sweat.

No one talked, much less laughed anymore. They just waited.

For *Whispercream.*

The new flavor had appeared three weeks ago. White. Creamy. Sweet and cold. Its scent lingered in your nostrils long after you'd walked away. People raved about it. Said it tasted like childhood. Like remembering something you never knew you wanted so badly.

At first, it was just the lines. But then people started disappearing.

Phones left at tables. Purses in wicker chairs. Hotel beds unslept in, sheets still tucked tight. Like their owners had evaporated mid-step, mid-thought. No screams. No violence. No blood. Just absence, and that attractive sugary scent hanging in the air.

Anne McNally, sixteen, watched from the upstairs window of the fudge shop. Her father, once loud, gruff, and red-faced, barely spoke anymore. His eyes gleamed under the fluorescents. He smiled a lot, but the smile never really showed in his eyes. Not much did anymore. He said the new flavor came to him in a dream. Strangely, he never let anyone else near the mixer anymore.

One night, Anne stood in the kitchen, pretending to clean. Beneath her feet, from between the floorboards, she heard it: very low, like a child singing inside a closet. "Ssstay . . . sssstay with meee. . . ."

The voice slithered up through the cracks. Anne dropped her sponge. A cooling tray on the counter began to tremble. The fudge on it shimmered, the surface rippling.

Anne touched it.

As soon as she did, scenes of horror flashed in her mind. Dark water. A small, pale hand. Then a muffled scream. She staggered back, heart thudding. Upstairs, her father hummed a lullaby in the wrong key.

At 2:00 a.m., Anne was compelled to explore and snuck downstairs, and in just a matter of a few steps, she approached a room in the basement. It was sealed with rusted chains and a sign that read:

OFF-LIMITS. DANGEROUS EQUIPMENT. DO NOT ENTER.

It was padlocked. Twice. She pulled out the bolt cutters and flashlight she'd tucked away earlier.

The door groaned open. The whispering returned, only louder now, and too close, as if someone were breathing into her ear. Her flashlight beam sliced through webs and dust. Cooling racks, slick with old fudge, leaned like tombstones. The stench of mold and rot lingered, thinly veiled by synthetic vanilla.

She went deeper in and stepped on a

waterlogged stuffed animal crawling with sugar ants. She hesitated, then stopped and sighed. She looked up. There was a wall, one newer than the rest. Its bricks were different, with sloppy mortar and a single, small handprint pressed into the center. Anne jammed a crowbar into the seam and pried. The bricks cracked and mortar crumbled. A cluster of earwigs crawled out, and she saw a room. Inside: dust-laden toys, a rotted doll's head, a pacifier melted into warped plastic, and an urn, small, porcelain, caked with dust. On it, written in a child's uneven scrawl: *For Daddy. Don't forget me.*

Its lid was cracked. Ashes spilled out, gray and white, like soiled powdered sugar. Her breath caught.

The whispering intensified. Anne turned and her flashlight flickered. And there stood a girl, no more than seven years old, her face ashen and her eyes deeply set, her lips smeared with fudge. So were her teeth. And so was the spoon clutched in her hand, small and silver. Her head sat atop her neck at an unnatural angle. Her limbs were weirdly long, bent, as if someone had forgotten how bones work and put her back together the wrong way.

Anne tried to speak.

The girl spoke instead. "It was cold in the lake. But Daddy brought me back. He said he'd make everyone remember me." She stepped closer. Bare feet left sticky fudge prints on the concrete. "They eat my bone dust now. I make them warm and safe and forever."

Anne stumbled backward, but the stairs were gone; the door sealed shut.

The girl raised the spoon. "I don't want to be alone anymore."

Anne screamed. The girl echoed it, not in fear, but in cruel delight. It sounded like ten voices screaming through one tiny throat. Some cried for help. Others begged for more. One voice sounded like her father.

Anne turned and ran into a wall that hadn't been there before. Every path led back to the urn. The toys. The girl.

Fudge began to slowly drip from the ceiling. It hissed where it touched her skin— burning *cold*. She fell, her palms sinking into the sticky substance, sucking at her hands like quicksand. The girl knelt beside her. "Just a taste," she whispered. "Then you'll know."

The spoon pressed against Anne's lips. She clenched her mouth shut.

The girl giggled. She did not sound like a child. "That's okay," she said. "You'll scream soon. And your mouth will open again."

McNally's Fudge Shop opened on time.

Tourists lined up early, eyes vacant with expectation. One woman gagged after her first bite, clutching her throat. Then she swallowed, followed by a smile.

The girl at the counter handed out samples, cheerful and glassy-eyed. She looked familiar.

No one noticed her hands were too cold.

No one noticed she never blinked.

No one noticed that every bite of Whispercream contained something that stirred, unseen, just beneath the tongue, revealing:

Remember me.

In the freezer, something moved.

It sounded like a child, humming through a mouthful of ice.

COME TO BED, MOMMY

DR. Susan Stoddard had spent twenty years cataloging and caring for the most delicate and dangerous arachnids on Earth. She believed spiders weren't to be feared—they were evolutionary miracles, creatures whose precision, elegance, and misunderstood grace had developed over untold millennia.

This summer, she took a sabbatical from the university to study invasive arachnids at the Detroit Zoo's Butterfly Garden and Insect House, among the most respected in the country.

That's why she screamed when Denny Caldwell, the Wayne State fullback doing community service for his college class, knocked over a container holding several

Araneus diadematus—garden spider—speci-mens. One spider had nearly been crushed beneath the wheel of the metal cart.

"You idiot!" Susan snapped, cradling the displaced orb weaver like a wounded bird. "Do you realize what you've done? These spiders are delicate."

Embarrassed and ashamed, Denny stammered an apology.

Susan held her palm to her forehead and sighed.

She returned home in Grosse Pointe Park just after four. Still affected by the Denny incident, she barely noticed the golden light streaming through the curtains of the house as she pulled into the drive. She paid the babysitter, then went to the bathroom to soak a cloth in cold water and wipe her face and the back of her neck before climbing the stairs to peek in on her seven-year-old daughter, Miriam, who lay sleeping.

At the sight of her daughter deep in sleep, Susan smiled. Then she saw it.

Loxosceles reclusa. A brown recluse, no doubt. It was motionless on the pale pink comforter, inches from Miriam's arm. Susan's breath caught. She'd handled funnel-webs, bark spiders, even a *Sicarius*, but this was her daughter's room. She moved without thinking. She had trained her hands to be still, precise, reverent. But in that moment, her fingers had acted on their own. She used the facecloth to grab the spider. Its body crumpled under her palm with a quick, wet crunch.

Miriam stirred but didn't wake.

Susan opened the cloth revealing the dead spider. Her heart thudded. She sighed. *It had been acting normally, not aggressive, she* thought. *It might not have even bitten her . . . I could've caught it. Brought it outside. But I'd killed it.*

An irrational fear had overridden everything she believed in. She wrapped it in a tissue, flushed it, and told herself it was over.

That night, while brushing her teeth, she saw another spider—a common house spider—on the ceiling. Bigger than usual. Much bigger. Tennis ball sized. In disbelief, she slowly backed out of the bathroom to retrieve her phone from her bedroom to capture an image of the anomaly.

She tiptoed back. By the time the camera focused, the thing was gone.

Shaking her head, she stood and checked every corner. Nothing. But the air felt colder, the room darker.

The next day, there were two more spiders in the kitchen. Hairy, large, and watching.

By the end of the week, they were everywhere. Her shoes. Behind the floor vents. The corners of every room. Always too large.

Susan stopped going to the Butterfly House and told the manager to take over the feedings. Denny called to check on her, leaving a voicemail when she didn't answer.

"Hello, Dr. Stoddard . . . uh, it's Denny and, uh, I just wanted to apologize again about that spider," he stopped and let out a deep breath. "I'm a klutz. Ask my coach. Anyway, I'm sorry and hope as soon as you get back you can forgive me. Bye."

By Sunday, the spiders were the size of cats. One crept across Susan's bedroom wall as she rocked Miriam to sleep. Its eight claws tapped rhythmically, audible in the quiet. Susan didn't scream. She only wept, cold and silent, rocking slowly, staring at the thing's eyes glinting in the dark.

On Tuesday night, she dreamed of webs. Endless webs stretching across her house. Tangled, sticky threads wrapping around her body, pulling her into the walls. She woke to the smell of spiders, dry rot, dust, and something older, earthier filled her nostrils. She rushed to Miriam's room. It was empty. The bed undisturbed. The window closed. No sign of struggle. Just a thin thread of silk winding out from the closet.

She threw open the door. Nothing. Behind her, she heard the soft brush of legs on wood. She turned. Again, nothing. Just beneath her skin, something twitched, not muscle, not a vein.

Something inside her moved.

The following night, Susan sat on the couch with a kitchen knife and a can of bug spray. The lights flickered. Her eyelids were unbearably heavy.

The spiders had grown again. One hung from the ceiling fan, swaying, watching. They were angry. She knew it. The first one—the brown recluse—had been a mother. They were punishing her.

She jolted awake to the sound of the basement door creaking open. Something vast began pulling itself up the stairs. The house groaned. Webs trembled like discordant cello strings.

Susan stood, knife raised. Eight legs gripped the banister. Its body glistened; its eyes gleamed. It was as large as a man. Its face held intelligence and cold hatred.

Then a giggle. Miriam's. "Sssstop, Mommy," she said, stepping from the shadows behind the spider. "You're scaring them."

Susan's hand dropped. "Miriam?"

Her daughter smiled. Her eyes glazed, multifaceted. They caught the flickering light and threw it back, not like eyes, but like polished stone. The spider loomed in front of her. Her hand caressed the top of its abdomen. Then, with a grace that felt human, it stepped aside. Miriam opened her arms. "Come to bed, Mommy."

Susan hesitated. Her feet stuck. The floor was thick with silk. But she didn't fight it. She took a step. Then another. Her breathing slowed. "I'm coming, baby," she whispered. Inside her, something shifted. A warmth, a serenity. The old muscles of fear unwound. Her hand let go of the knife, and it clattered on the floor. A strand of silk gently curled around her wrist. Another brushed her cheek, as if guiding her.

Again, from beneath her skin, something moved. Like wings unfolding after a molt. She reached her daughter and knelt.

Miriam wrapped her tiny arms around her mother's neck. Her breath smelled of dust and earth. "You're not mad anymore?"

Susan closed her eyes. "No," she said. "I remember now."

Behind them, the spider clicked softly and began to weave.

Outside, morning broke. Denny pedaled up the walk, a paper sack of donuts dangling from his handlebars. He knocked on the door, rang the bell. No answer. "Dr. Stoddard?" he called. "It's me, Denny. Just . . . checkin' in. I bought some donuts."

The air felt off, still, too quiet. He shifted weight from foot to foot. "Hello?"

He turned to leave, then stopped. Something made him glance up.

In the upstairs window, two shapes stood behind a gauzy curtain. A girl and a woman. Both watching. Both smiling.

Then, from behind the woman, something moved. A mass, like a shadow, a shape. Grotesque, suspended upside down from the ceiling.

Denny dropped the sack and ran, the donuts spilled and rolled across the sidewalk.

From behind the curtain, Miriam watched him go. "He's funny," she said.

"He'll come back," Susan whispered. "We'll wait."

Miriam grinned, followed by a clicking from her throat. "Yes. And when he does, I'll help spin."

AUNT GINNY'S UNDEAD

IT had been just over a week since Great Aunt Ginny died.

Her great nephew, Bruce Colston, stepped off the first Mackinac Island ferry of the day. The dock was slick with remnants of last night's rain. His father had gone ahead to handle the will. His mother and little sister were stranded in Cheboygan with a dead car battery. That left fifteen-year-old Bruce the man of the cottage.

The island carriage driver pulled up thirty feet from the gate and stopped. "I ain't going farther," he said, flicking the reins. He reached into his coat and pulled out a small bundle of cedar twigs wrapped in rawhide string, tossing it to Bruce. "This here's a *manito* charm.

It might keep the restless at bay for a little while." He flicked the reins again. "You won't make it till morning without it."

Bruce unwrapped the bundle, inhaling the sharp scent of sweetgrass and cedar. "Manito?"

"The spirits that live here," the driver said, eyes dark beneath his hat. "Your Aunt Ginny knew the island's old ways. The Thirteenth Chime ain't just a family curse. It's a warning. The island doesn't forget debts."

The house had no electricity. The generator in the shed was rusted to death. Bruce wandered the quiet halls by candlelight. Shadows bounced across the walls. Family portraits followed him with their eyes. Aunt Ginny's portrait, once above the fireplace, was missing. In its place was a smear of black soot.

Bruce tried sleeping on the couch, but the grandfather clock wouldn't stop ticking. At midnight, it struck thirteen times. The final chime sounded strangely off, almost wet, like a stone dropped in a deep pool of blood. Frost webbed the inside of the windows. Bruce's breath fogged before vanishing completely. Somewhere upstairs, a rocking chair creaked. No one was allowed to touch it. "It faces the window for a reason," Aunt Ginny said last summer.

Bruce climbed the stairs and stopped outside her room. The door hung open. Inside, the chair rocked, facing the corner. He stepped in, scanning the room, and his eyes landed on a small leather-bound journal lying on the bedside table. He picked it up and flipped through its damp pages, stopping on one:

The Thirteenth Chime does more than haunt our bloodline; it marks the breaking of an ancient promise with the Manitou, the spirit of endless hunger, good, and evil. Long ago, our ancestors shook the sacred grounds where the Manitou sleeps, and the price was set in blood. Each chime tightens the noose, wearing down the soul until the Manitou's hunger is satisfied.

Bruce froze as he read the final paragraph:

Only the blood of the Colstons can bind it once more. But it must be willing. The mirrors were the cage, and now the cage has cracked.

The phone rang. He snatched it up. His own voice screamed through the receiver: "Don't open the cellar door! Don't—" static swallowed the rest. Then came a knock from beneath the floorboards. Bruce stepped into the basement, flashlight in one hand, the manito charm in the other. The walls were lined with canning jars filled with teeth. He paused, clutching the cedar bundle tighter.

Behind him, glass cracked. He turned. The mirror on the far wall split. From it, a mix of voices spoke: his sister, his mother, Aunt Ginny, all begging. Then his own: "Let me in."

He ran, but as he did, the house shifted, hallways stretching and walls closing in. Before he could reach the door at the other end, the floor opened up, sending him tumbling into the parlor. The air, thick and rotten, cocooned him. Fear paralyzed him.

As he contemplated giving up hope, the manito charm burned like a hot coal in his pocket. With a gasp, he yanked it out and drove it into the nearest mirror. The resulting explosion wasn't just a sound; it was pressure, as if the air had been shoved inside out. The walls bled white light. Portraits screamed and caught fire. Bruce ran until he couldn't, until his lungs failed and his legs gave out, finally collapsing on the bluff just before dawn.

The cold was gone. The sky was pale and blue. The house behind him sat silent and still, untouched by flame. A family pedaled by on bicycles.

"Do you know the Colston house?" Bruce asked the family, his voice hoarse.

They blinked. "Sorry," said the woman.

Later, at the island's edge, Bruce found an old woman weaving a basket of cedar strips beneath a towering pine. Her eyes were sharp and ancient.

"You carry the weight of the broken promise," she said without looking up.

Bruce held out Aunt Ginny's journal. "Do you know about the Thirteenth Chime?"

She nodded slowly. "Your family was given a gift and a curse. The island is alive with the Manitou's breath, and it remembers. Your Aunt Ginny kept the spirit at bay with her strength and respect for the old ways. But the bloodline must choose now."

"Choose what?"

"To honor the pact or be consumed. The manito will guide you, but you must listen to the land, not just fear it."

Bruce swallowed his fear. "How?"

"Follow the cedar's path. Face the hunger before the next chime."

Bruce caught his own haggard reflection in a shop window later that day. But there was something wrong with it.

It smiled and waved, and motioned for him to follow.

VOICES CALLING AT BRITISH LANDING

ETHAN slammed the back door behind him, ignoring his mother's muffled shouts. The countryside was supposed to be *healing*, but to Ethan, it felt like being buried alive in open air.

There were no streetlights, no sirens, no horns. Just trees—endless trees—and the constant hum of bugs. Boredom, anxiety, and silence thickened around him. The wind tasted odd, old and metallic, like rust scraped off a coffin nail.

He pedaled fast, mud pellets flinging from

his tires as he veered off the road and onto a narrow trail. The woods rose around him like a forgotten cathedral, branches like claws, trunks leaning in too close.

Slow and steady, the clouds crept in.

One second the trail was clear, and the next, it vanished into a thick gray mist. His front tire struck something but didn't bounce; instead, it *crunched.*

Ethan flew forward. The world spun. The ground slammed into his ribs, stealing his breath. For a moment, he saw stars, and then nothing. When he came to, everything was quiet.

Until the voices with British accents. All of them urgent, clipped, and angry.

Shapes moved between the trees—long coats, heavy boots, muskets. Soldiers. Pale, hollow-eyed faces blurred like ash in water. One turned to him. "I beseech thee . . . return only at the midnight hour."

Then, they vanished.

The crash had startled Ethan, and he still had a dull pain in his head, but he shook it off. *It might have been a concussion,* he told himself. *A hallucination.* But something in his gut said otherwise. So, he returned every night, right around midnight.

And every night, the haze thickened.

The same flickers of battle repeated, muzzle flashes lighting up skeletal faces, bayonets plunging, screams that drilled straight into his bones. Gunpowder, blood, and dust filled the air.

And always, the drumbeat. *Boom . . . Boom . . . Brr-rrr-oom.* Like a heartbeat being dragged into the grave.

By the fourth night, Ethan couldn't pretend it was a dream anymore. He woke in bed filthy, his shoes muddy, leaves in the sheets. Once, he found a warped bullet in his coat pocket, warm to the touch and streaked with red.

One evening when he was picking up some snacks at the gas station, he asked an old cashier if he'd ever seen the haze. The man's face went pale. His hands shook. "Fog like that don't roll in by weather; fog like that's made," he said. "You keep walking into it, you'll walk it forever."

The next time Ethan saw the haze, it came to meet him.

It poured from the trees like smoke from a battlefield. The battlefield scene replayed again, only worse. A soldier with half a face dragged himself through the mud, whispering to a corpse. Another screamed while firing wildly into nothing before disappearing with a puff of smoke. The air throbbed with death. Suddenly, soldiers began to notice him.

They *recognized* him.

Heads snapped toward him like marionettes. One whispered his name. Another raised a bayonet and pointed. Ethan ran.

Deep into the woods, he found a maple tree, split long ago by lightning. In the hollow, something waited: a fraying satchel with rusted buttons, a British soldier's yellowing journal tucked inside. The final pages were smeared, but one passage still bled through:

"Thornton abandoned his command. Trapped in slaughter. His curse binds us, but death will not accept us. The boy's drum beats steady. We still march. We still burn."

Scrawled at the bottom: *Do not follow the drum.*

As the clock struck twelve, the scene unfolded again. But this time, Ethan saw himself: his hoodie, his bike. His double was watching the battle like he'd never left. The loop had folded him in. And now, all the ghostly voices called one name. His.

He didn't sleep. He researched. He found an old map from a basement sale at Ste. Anne Church marked in red: *LOST*. The journals spoke of one soul never buried, never remembered. A drummer, a boy killed during a charge who died alone.

Hours later, in the dark of night, Ethan didn't run. He walked into the haze. Gunfire ripped the sky. Ghosts sprinted past. Blood misted the trees. He followed the beat— deeper, deeper—until he found the hollow. There lay the boy, small, curled. His fingers still wrapped around drumsticks. His skull crushed. His mouth locked in a silent scream.

Ethan knelt beside the ghost, its eyes wide, trembling.

"I know," Ethan said softly. "You were alone."

The ghost turned. Tears streaked his transparent cheeks.

"I'll stay," Ethan whispered. "No one forgets you now." He crawled into the hollow.

Mud gripped his limbs like cold hands. His breath slowed. The ghost reached out—

And the drumbeat stopped.

Gunfire froze. Bayonets halted mid-thrust. All the soldiers turned their heads toward the hollow. For the first time in 247 years, the loop paused. Ethan's heart slowed and the fog receded. A voice brushed his ear, soft and solemn: "You were seen."

Then, darkness.

Search teams came. Helicopters, dogs, floodlights. They found his bike and his folded hoodie by the maple. His shattered phone, screen still glowing: 12:17 a.m.

Ethan was never found. Some say he ran. Some say the forest took him. But if you're near British Landing on a fog-heavy night, and your phone loses signal, and your breath turns cold, don't follow the drum. Don't follow the voices, and don't look too long into the trees, because if you do, you might see a terrified kid watching the battle unfold.

That kid might already be you.

STORM MAIDEN

I T was the cheesiest ferry on Lake Huron, and everybody knew it.

Painted saddle brown with red sails and plastic cannons, the *Storm Maiden* was more tourist trap than transportation. But on a chilly October evening, with a dense fog rolling in, the joke wore thin.

The Halloween Pirate Cruise was supposed to be fun, with pirate trivia, cider, and glow-in-the-dark plastic swords. For thirteen-year-old Natalie, her cousin Dean, and a dozen other kids in eye patches and dollar store bandanas, it had started that way.

Until the fog came.

"Should we even be out here?" Dean whispered, gripping the railing. "I can't see the island. I can't see *anything*."

"It's fine," Natalie said, trying to sound braver than she felt. "They do this every year. It's probably part of the show."

The fog was thick as wool. Waves slapped against the hull in a nervous rhythm. The crew—two local college guys in pirate coats—had stopped goofing around and were now speaking to the captain in low, tense voices.

"I don't think it's supposed to be this real," Dean said. "Look at their faces."

The captain, an old man named Reilly with a plastic parrot on his shoulder, suddenly cut the engine. Silence dropped like a curtain. "We've got a bit of a . . . visibility issue," he called out. "Everybody stay calm. Just drifting for a bit till the fog lifts."

But the fog didn't lift. It thickened.

A shape appeared in the haze, vast, black, and still. It was the silhouette of a ship.

"That . . . that's not one of the Star Line boats," Natalie murmured.

"No," Dean said, backing away from the rail. "It's *huge*."

The shape moved. Boards groaned. The water roiled. A dark sail creaked in the still air. Lanterns flickered to life, green fire that didn't look like any electricity.

And then the whining of ropes and a splash followed by a sound like claws on wood.

"They're boarding us," someone whispered.

A figure emerged from the fog. Not a man, a *thing*, dressed in rotted rags, soaked in lake water, eyes glowing green through the holes of a soggy tricorn hat. His jaw hung too low, like it had been broken and never healed right.

"Permission to come aboard," it burbled, voice thick with water.

Screams broke out. Kids shoved toward the center of the deck.

Dean grabbed Natalie's hand. "Run!"

"Where?!"

Another figure climbed over the side, then another. Their skin was rotted, their flesh bloated. Some had skeletal hands gripping rusted cutlasses. One dragged a chain wrapped around a life vest, still dripping blood.

"These aren't actors," Natalie said. "Dean, they're freaking *real*."

The ghost captain stepped forward, his eyes glowing like deep-sea lava.

"Stolen waters," he said. "You mocked the grave. Now you sail with us."

Captain Reilly took a step back, fumbling for his flare gun. He raised it up and fired, its light streaking red into the fog. It fizzled out in the inky blackness. One of the ghost crew lunged and dragged him screaming over the rail.

Dean and Natalie ran below deck, searching for a place to hide.

But the belly of the ship was even worse. The party decorations, plastic bones and skeletons, were twitching. One of them jerked its head toward Natalie. "Go no farther," it croaked.

Heeding its warning, they slammed the hatch shut and ran to the wheelhouse.

The fog pressed against the windows, swirling with a malicious intelligence. Like it was *watching*.

The radio hissed with static. "This is the *Storm Maiden*! We're under attack! We need help!" Natalie screamed into the mic.

A voice answered from the radio speaker,

wet and slow. "Too late. This ship already sails beyond."

Dean pointed toward the bow. "The chain, they're tying us to their ship. They're gonna tow us into the fog forever!"

Natalie grabbed a fire axe from the emergency glass. "Then we cut the chain."

They fought through the suffocating cloud, swinging at hideous grasping hands. Natalie reached the bow and saw the thick, blackened chain linking their ferry to the ghost ship. It pulsed like a vein.

She raised the axe and brought it down. Sparks flew.

The ghost captain let out a piercing wail that drilled into her skull. The ferry lurched.

Natalie put all her strength into another strike. The chain snapped. Instantly, the fog puffed and scattered. Light broke through . . . real sunlight!

The *Storm Maiden* bobbed alone on still waters. No more ghost ship, no crew, no weird green eyes.

Captain Reilly and the others were gone. Natalie, Dean, and three sobbing kids clung to each other on the deck.

Later, the Coast Guard found them adrift. The crew had "fallen overboard," they said.

Tragic accident. Fog confusion. But Natalie knew better.

Somewhere out there in the gray, between the worlds, the dead still sailed.

ZOMBIE SEAGULLS

LOGAN stepped off the Mackinac Island ferry and into the combined aromas of fudge, lake water, horse dung, and pine.

Tourists jostled past him, snapping selfies with bags of taffy and melting ice cream cones. No cars. No honking. Only the clop of hooves and jingling of bridle chains.

And gulls. Always gulls. Vociferous, foraging, selfish gulls.

As a self-taught artist, Logan had spent countless hours sketching the squawking maniacs: fat, feathered, greedy creatures that stalked tourists for french fries and wailed like banshees to pick apart dropped hot dogs and pizza crust. But not today.

Today, the gulls were oddly silent. Dozens

lined the ferry terminal roof, still as statues . . . watching.

Logan slowed.

"Logan!" Aunt Marla's voice rang out from her fudge shop's delivery cart. She waved a gloved hand. "Let's go, kiddo! There's tourists to fatten up!"

He hesitated. One of the gulls jerked its head in a twitchy, unnatural motion and stared straight at him. Its eye was cloudy. Not blind, just off. Logan blinked. The gull blinked too, scratched its feathers, looked away. *Just me*, Logan thought. But the goosebumps all over him told the truth: He was creeped out.

That evening, golden light spilled down Main Street as shops shuttered and bikes pedaled past. Aunt Marla ladled hot caramel onto a tray of fudge. Logan stepped outside, wiping his hands on his apron. A wind from off the water cooled his face.

The gulls were still there, on every roof, chimney, and post, but now they all faced the lake. Every single one. A dull thud cracked the silence. Across the street, a gull fell from the sky like a dropped brick. Wings splayed. Neck twisted.

Logan ran over. "Holy crap."

The bird twitched. Its feet kicked. Its body spasmed, then rose. Its left wing hung oddly low. Its neck was bent at an impossible angle. Still, it turned to face him. Its eyes were dead-fish gray. And then—somehow— it flew. Unsteady, broken, but purposeful, it headed back toward the rooftops.

Aunt Marla leaned out the door. "What was that?"

"A gull. It crashed. I thought it died, but it didn't."

"Probably just sick. Don't get close, you'll catch the bird flu."

"I didn't touch it," he said. "It flew away. With a crooked neck."

"Even more reason to stay away." She stepped inside, the screen door slamming shut behind her.

Logan didn't move. His fingers itched for his sketchbook. Something was wrong with the seagulls. Perfect to capture in a sketch.

By the third day, Logan had filled five pages. Gulls with blank eyes. Talons like hooks. Wings held stiffly, braced against something other than wind. And always—*always*—silent.

On Tuesday night, soft tapping woke him from sleep. He crept upstairs. At the attic window, a single gull stood in the moonlight, pecking, not frantic, but deliberate. One . . . two . . . three times. It tilted its head, watching.

He drew it the next morning, his hands trembling. After breakfast, he biked to the old cemetery near Fort Mackinac, where tall grass swallowed forgotten headstones. The gulls were there too. Circling, watching.

He was startled by rustling leaves behind him, followed by a voice. "You shouldn't be here after dark."

Logan turned. A boy, around his age, stood at the gate. Hoodie, jeans, a long black braid tied with red thread.

"So who are you, and why are you here?" Logan asked.

The boy stepped closer. "Name's Jonah. Because this is where they come. The spirits and the gulls."

Logan stopped to consider the boy's

words, then he frowned. "What does it have to do with you?"

"My family's from the U.P. We're renting a cottage for a week. My grandfather used to tell stories about this place. He was different. Worked as a carriage tour driver here a long time ago. Told me stories about spirits on Mackinac." He glanced at Logan's sketchbook and nodded. "You've seen the change, the gulls, haven't you?"

Logan hesitated. "Yeah. It's . . . not normal."

"I've seen them too."

A voice from across the road interrupted. "You guys ghost-hunting or bird-watching?"

A girl walked across and leaned over the fence. Tall, tan, a bleached streak in her ponytail. "I'm Maya," she said. "My sister's doing this dumb ghost vlog. You probably saw her livestream yesterday."

Logan blinked. "You mean The Girl on the Cliff?" He laughed. "I heard she screamed when a spider hit her ring light. Kind of fake."

"But she disappeared," Jonah said.

Maya's smirk faded. "What?"

"After the stream cut out," Jonah said. "Did she come back?"

Maya shook her head slowly. "No . . . She texted that she was editing at the lighthouse. Then nothing."

They exchanged uneasy glances.

Jonah broke the silence. "We gotta find out what's going on."

Logan pointed skyward at several gulls circling. "And I think it starts with them."

Jonah led them through the woods behind the fort, his voice low. "Mackinac wasn't always a tourist trap. Grandpa said this was Anishinaabe land. The Great Spirit moved in the wind and sky. But during the wars, soldiers dug up burial sites. Tossed bones in pits. Paved over sacred ground."

Logan's voice was barely a whisper. "You think the gulls are like possessed?"

"Not exactly," Jonah said. "Maybe they're messengers. And something is waking up. I want to show you something I discovered by accident yesterday."

They followed him into town, behind the fudge shop, to a dumpster labeled "Doud House Renovation." Bones—long, thin, *human*—lay in the trash.

"Oh my God," Maya said, gagging. "That's a femur."

Jonah picked up a rib fragment. "I was riding through here and saw these and stopped, thinking they were too weird looking to be steak or chicken bones. They dumped them like garbage. I also found this." He reached into his pocket and removed an unfolded, tattered sheet and carefully opened it. It was a faded pencil sketch of the fort grounds and written in messy cursive was the word "catacomb," with an arrow pointing to one of the fort buildings.

A shriek tore through the air above. Three gulls dove. One slammed into a shutter and dropped, twitching. Its eyes were milkywhite. Its beak opened—no sound escaped.

"We need shelter," Maya said, backing away.

Logan held up his key. "Fudge shop."

That night, the gulls came. Windows cracked. Talons scraped shingles. Maya screamed as a gull burst through the attic vent, body jerking like a snake. Gulls invaded the fudge shop. Feathers fell like fake snow.

Sensing this was the moment to escape,

they were forced to flee back outside and into the street. Wings filled the sky. What looked like marbles rolled across the pavement, until Logan saw them clearly. Eyeballs, all of them. Hazy and human.

By morning, the island was cut off. No ferries were running. The power went out. Phones died. Tourists panicked. Some tried to escape on kayaks. A couple vanished near Arch Rock—only paddles remained. At Mission Point, a hotel worker stood frozen, gulls perched around her. When a guest called her name, she turned. Her face twisted. She shrieked like a gull, then ran, clawing at the air, into the trees.

"It's not just birds," Logan said. "It's spreading."

"Infection?" Maya asked.

"Not sickness," Jonah said. "Possession. It's as if the air remembers what was done here. And it's using the gulls."

At dusk, they walked to Fort Mackinac. They stopped at a cedar tree. Jonah pulled a handful of cedar needles and placed them in his pocket.

"What's that for?"

"Grampa said they purify, make things safe. Might as well bring some."

They continued on. Gulls lined the walls and cannons, watching.

Jonah removed the tattered sheet he'd shown Logan and Maya the day before. It led them to a large wooden building on the fort parade grounds, with a cellar entrance built into its limestone foundation, its doors marked "Closed for Structural Safety." Carefully, they entered and climbed down the stairs. Logan pulled on a string and lights went on.

Inside there were bones, lots of them, all wrapped in rotted cloth. There were skulls with teeth, beads, buttons, old uniform fragments.

"We can't leave them like this," Logan whispered.

Jonah nodded. "We won't."

The sky was calm and heavy with low clouds. They carried the remains in pillowcases, wrapped in fudge shop linens. Jonah pulled the cedar needles from his pocket and broke them into pieces, sprinkling them in a ring, and placed the bones gently inside.

He uttered the names carved into nearby stones. "Mukwa. Nodin. Miskwa."

The gulls came, hundreds of them, circling slowly, then landing. And, one by one, they formed a perfect ring around the ritual site facing inward. When the final bone rested within the circle, the air trembled. An explosion of bird cries shook the trees, the stones, the very ground.

Then, quiet.

The gulls lifted as one. Broke into the clouds. Some flew toward the woods, others toward the water.

One remained. It landed in front of Logan and tilted its head, its eyes still pale. It cawed once, then rose and vanished into the sky.

A week later, the ferries returned along with the tourists. The fudge shop reopened. People blamed a solar flare for the crisis. No one mentioned the bones—maybe they didn't want to scare away the tourists. Maya's sister appeared with no memory of what happened. Together, they left with their parents. Jonah vanished without a goodbye. Logan packed his sketchbook into his duffel.

As he arrived at the dock, preparing to leave, he looked up. A single gull circled the lighthouse, its wings shimmering in the sun.

A white feather drifted down and landed at his feet.

Logan stared at it for a long time.

SKULL CAVE

FOG rolled in fast from the straits, clouding Mackinac Island in an eerie quiet. The treetops stilled, their trunks stiff like sentinels holding their breath. It was August, but the wet air was cold enough to make you shiver.

Alex trailed behind the island's popular "ghost tour," hands shoved deep in his hoodie pocket. His earbuds stayed in place but turned off so no one would bother him. He was on the island visiting his grandparents for a "quiet week," which really meant no Wi-Fi, no phone signal, and no one under seventy. Cruel and unusual punishment for a fifteen-year-old.

The group stopped before a jagged cave mouth carved deep into the rock. "Skull

Cave," the guide said, tapping his cane against the outer cave wall. He was tall and thin, with long gray hair pulled into a loose man bun. "British soldiers once found this cave filled with the bones of native warriors. They kept their own dead here too. People say if you step inside and listen close," he cupped his hand near his ear, "the cave talks back."

A few kids laughed. One girl spat out her gum and snapped a selfie. Alex didn't smile. The cave exhaled a cold breath smelling of wet stone and dried urine.

As the group started to move on, Alex hesitated. He knew the way back to town and had already tuned out the dorky ghost guide. Stepping inside, he pulled out his pocket flashlight. Its beam cut through the creeping dark, glinting off the slick, uneven cave walls. With each step deeper, the air grew colder. His phone lost signal almost immediately. His "quiet week" had truly begun, and he was alone.

A few yards in, the ground sloped steeply downward. He stopped, peering into the blackness, feeling as if something beyond his sight was tugging at him, as if the cave didn't want him to leave. He turned to go back and his foot slipped. Stone scraped his hands as he fell, tumbling into silence. His flashlight bounced away, its beam spinning wildly before vanishing. He landed hard; pain flared in his shoulder.

The air was heavy and dry. Alex sat up and held his breath. He'd fallen into a chamber. He moved his hands around in the dark, and they touched hard, cold objects, some smooth, others jagged. His fingers touched a kind of fabric, perhaps old clothing, he thought. Beyond this, there was nothing else for him to do but call out for help, which he did for some time until his voice cracked and his head ached. Before long, he lay on the crumbled ground and fell asleep.

Alex's eyes opened to a dimly lit chamber. It must have been morning, he thought. The objects he'd been touching weren't rocks or stones, but bones, and they weren't scattered around haphazardly. They were arranged. Spines curved like ribbed rivers across the floor. Skulls were stacked into perfect pyramids. Long bones were fanned out like wings. Carved into the walls were symbols, sharp, deep, ancient, strange. Alex stood still, careful not to disturb anything. But the bones shifted. A skull rolled to his foot. Then another. Then voices—breathy, strange mutterings—echoed all around him, behind, above, inside his head.

The symbols pulsed faintly. Hearing something behind him, Alex turned. A tall figure rose from the center of the room, not stepping out of the bones, but forming from them. Its shape rippled like smoke, eyes burning red and unblinking. Its voice was dry and deep, as if spoken through dust. "Will you stand for us?"

Alex backed away. "I—I didn't mean—" His voice cracked. "I'm not supposed to— this was a mistake."

The voices grew louder. Shadows shifted. The symbols flared brighter. The figure raised a skeletal hand and slowly reached out and extended its boney forefinger and lightly dragged the tip of its fingernail along Alex's arm. "One step. One word. That is all it takes."

Alex turned to run. His foot landed inside a faint circle of ash etched into the floor. The moment he touched it, everything froze. The morning light vanished, the voices stopped, and the figure dissolved. He was alone in the dark again, but something had awakened.

Weeks of searching turned into months. Drones swept the skies. Dogs tracked. But Alex was never found. Skull Cave changed. People said the air around it grew foul. Phones died near its mouth. Some tourists even fainted. Others left crying for no reason. Occasionally, people claimed they heard a voice, one not spoken aloud, but inside their heads.

"Go back. You don't belong here."

And every now and then someone disappeared.

One evening, nearly a year later, another boy—curious, bored, alone—slipped away from a group tour. He stepped into Skull Cave before sunset, just as a fog began rolling in. He never heard the wind stop. He never noticed the woods fall silent. He didn't see the pale ash circle until he stepped directly into it.

Far below, Alex opened his eyes. No longer white, they were red. The bones around him stirred again. And from somewhere deep inside, something that might have once been a boy called out: "One more."

Up above the fog thickened. The boy never walked back out.

But the thing wearing his skin did.

PIECES OF MADAME

THE Mackinac Island History Museum stood solemn and silent, its walls steeped in centuries of layered secrets.

Emma Taylor had volunteered at the museum for three weeks, mostly guiding tourists through exhibits on fur trading and early settlers. She liked the quiet, the sense of history, even the creaky floors. But her favorite part was the long, strange stories she coaxed out of the island's older staff. She was fascinated by legends and lore of the island. And no legend chilled her bones like the newest exhibit: the brittle remains of Madame LaFrambois.

"Stay clear of the LaFrambois exhibit after sundown, if you know what's good for you," muttered Mr. Marten, the elderly night guard, as he passed her on her second Tuesday working. He didn't stop walking.

"Why? You think the ghost is real?" she teased, trying to sound braver than she felt.

"Don't joke about that woman, girl. Some bones are best left buried." His voice faded as he turned the corner.

There was something deeply unsettling about Madame LaFrambois's bones. The glass case was enormous and sealed tight, resting on a carved oak base etched with strange symbols. The fragmented bones had been arranged meticulously, but something about them felt strange.

The air around the case was always icy cold, the kind of cold that crawled beneath your skin.

Earlier that day, Emma cornered Ms. Pierce, the museum curator, in her office. "Who donated Madame LaFrambois's remains, anyway?" she asked, feigning casual curiosity. "I thought she was buried under St. Anne's."

Ms. Pierce glanced up from her paperwork, eyes wary. "They were recovered, partially. A restoration team did the exhumation last winter. It was, let's say, controversial."

"Controversial how?"

"Some say we shouldn't have moved her. Local legend nonsense. That her death was abrupt and odd. That she cursed the land." She sighed. "But bones are just bones, Emma. This is history. Not ghost stories." The curator tried to make her feel better with a smile. It didn't work.

Emma had heard the stories shared by islanders. Centuries ago, Madame LaFrambois was a feared and respected trader. She died a violent death at the hands of those she trusted; it was said her body never found peace. For years, her remains had rested in a concrete crypt beneath the outdoor chapel at Ste. Anne Church. The locals warned that disturbing her bones would bring ruin, but the museum dismissed such talk as superstition.

One night after closing, Emma couldn't help but linger near the exhibit, the silence thickening around her. She peered at the bones, her breath fogging up the glass. She exhaled a sigh of release and began to turn away.

A hand pressed against the glass, thin, withered, veiny, its fingernails black, cracked, and jagged. The hand slowly scraped downward, leaving a smear of thick, dark blood.

Emma stumbled back, her heart pounding in her throat. A dry, raspy voice called in her ear, curdling her blood: "Bring me back . . . bring me back." She spun around, but the gallery was empty. The fluorescent lights flickered once, then steadied.

She ran home, convincing herself that stress and exhaustion were responsible for the voice she heard. But whatever had awoken that night in the museum followed her home. Night after night, ghastly beings chased her through her dreams, jolting her awake, drenched in sweat, the stench of death and decay thick in her nostrils.

Emma decided to visit the library to search for answers. Ms. Dorsett, the ancient librarian, had lowered her voice to a near-whisper when Emma asked about Madame LaFrambois.

"You should leave those bones alone, dear. She was betrayed by her own kin. Died with fire in her mouth and hatred in her eyes."

"You think she's really still around?"

"I know she is. My mother said she used to whisper from the chapel walls when the moon was high. You return what was taken, or she'll come collecting."

Emma laughed nervously, but Ms. Dorsett didn't smile.

At morning, Emma prepared to go to work, her reflection twisted in the mirror, and behind her stood a woman: hollow black eyes staring through her, skin torn away to reveal cracked bone, lips split and chapped. "Bring me back . . . ," rasped the voice from the glass, a cold breath brushing the back of Emma's neck.

Days later, Emma's neighbor vanished. Police found his body deep in the forest, his scalp torn back like a ripped canvas, bloody and raw. His eyes were fixed wide, frozen in terror. No one could explain what had happened.

The island's elderly librarian wasted away overnight. Her skin turned gray and dull, peeling like a molting lizard, her eyes sunken until only pinpricks of white remained. A low moan echoed through the rooms of her house as she died a lingering, lonely, and perplexing death.

Paranoia gnawed away at Emma. Strangers seemed to stare at her as she passed; shadows followed her at the edge of her vision; incessant scratching resonated under her floorboards. Her friends—perhaps out of fear—stopped answering her calls.

Finally, Emma couldn't take it anymore, and she cornered Ms. Pierce in the museum.

"You know something, don't you?" Emma demanded. "Something's wrong. That thing in the museum, it's not just a display. People are dying."

Ms. Pierce waved her into her office, locked the door behind them, and lowered the blinds. Her hands trembled as she pulled out a folder and laid a yellowed letter on the desk. Emma walked up and without touching the letter, read it:

December 3rd, 1802
Island, Michigan Territory

To whom it may concern—

I write this in grave secrecy and under considerable duress. I fear I may not long remain on this earth, for I have seen what should never walk again.

The woman LaFrambois—respected trader, widow, benefactor, and, I now believe, practitioner of the forbidden—was buried this fortnight beneath St. Anne's Chapel, though not in peace. Her body was not whole when we laid her to rest. Two ribs, her left hand, and a portion of her jaw were stolen prior to burial by men who feared her power and sought to break her hold on this land. They believed it would silence her forever.

Instead, it has cursed us.

In the nights since, I have heard her voice in the chapel rafters, low and bitter, calling for what was taken. Candles light without flame, stones bleed, and worse, the floorboards tremble as if bearing the weight of an unseen traveler.

I have buried the missing parts beneath the crypt's eastern wall, sealed in iron and wrapped in scripture, as my ancestors once did for the restless dead in the old country. But I do not know if it is enough. The body must be made whole, or the curse cannot be undone.

If you find this letter, I beg you: Do not disturb her again. Do not move her bones, lest you wake the one who never truly slept.

May God have mercy on us all.

— Father Henri Duval
Chaplain, St. Anne's Parish
Mackinac Island
December 3rd, 1802

Emma looked up, her mouth open, her eyes still.

Ms. Pierce met Emma's gaze. "We already opened the door," she said. "She's not just a ghost anymore. She's awake, and she's angry."

The air turned unbearably cold as she neared the final stretch to the museum—a biting frost crept beneath her skin, cooling her blood. Shadows stretched unnaturally, contorting into faces with hollow eyes and mouths twisted in silent screams.

In the museum, she bypassed the locked doors and hurried down dark halls. Her blood ran cold when she opened the case and grabbed the bones. She knew what she had to do. Heart hammering like a war drum, she hurried to return to the crypt.

Just as she rounded the corner at Marquette Park, an island police officer approached. Emma had seen him before but didn't know him, as he was new to the island. His face looked concerned. "Are you alright?" he asked.

Emma labored for words. "Just working late at the museum. Nothing to worry about."

Officer Riley raised an eyebrow at Emma's hand clutching the bones. "Whatcha got there?"

Emma dug deep to find a fake laugh. "Oh, yes, just some bones."

At that the officer stepped back, half-laughed, and nodded. "Well, all that archaeology stuff is beyond me. Just wanted to be sure you were okay."

"Yes. Thank you, sir, I appreciate that. Good night."

"Be careful and good night to you."

Emma ventured to the chapel and realized she'd left her flashlight at the museum, forced to work with only the moon to provide any light. She grunted as she slid back the con-crete slab covering the crypt. The air inside was rank with rot, sickening her lungs. From within, ghostly wails erupted. "Beneath . . . beneath . . . they lie beneath."

Nervously, she dug her hands into the soil beneath the crypt. Her fingers brushed something cold and hard. She dug deeper, feeling around, pulling out a small, steel box no larger than a purse. The latch fell away. She pulled off the top and squinted her eyes to see the contents.

Inside, wrapped in tattered Bible pages, lay Madame's missing bones. She raised the pages up so to see them in the moonlight. Barely legible painted words warned: "These remains must never be separated. Forever ill will and death will ensue whoever separates them."

Kneeling at the mound, Emma peeled back the cloth and laid the bones alongside the others. The brittle fragments shifted, aligning with an eerie position, as though some ancient instinct guided them. A low vibration rippled through the ground; the symbols etched into the crypt began to glow and the air filled with sulfuric cold evil.

A skeletal hand shot up from the dirt, and another one joined it and then another, clutching Emma's ankles and then her waist.

"You should have left me dead," a raspy voice sounded in Emma's mind, as though Madame LaFrambois spoke within.

A sudden, shaky beam of light cast on Emma.

"Hey!" Officer Riley hollered. He charged forward, eyes wide at the nightmarish scene, and lunged, grabbing Emma under her arms. "Hang on, I got you."

The hands fought back, but with a final exhausting pull, Riley dragged her out just as the soil collapsed inward with a deafening crack. Everything became still, the screaming was now silence.

The skeletal remains in the mound had settled—whole at last—and lay eerily peaceful.

A week later, Emma stood at the edge of the museum lawn, wrapped in a coat, sipping lukewarm tea. Officer Riley joined her, glancing at the now-closed chapel in the distance.

"She's back where she belongs," Emma said. "It's over."

Riley raised an eyebrow. "You sure about that?"

"She got what she wanted," Emma said. "Her bones are whole. The curse is gone."

Riley shrugged. "I hope so. I'll never forget what I saw, and I hope I never do again."

During the night the wind howled through the streets of Mackinac Island. At the museum, security alarms blared, but no one responded. The lights flickered, and then failed entirely. Inside, behind the locked glass case that once held Madame LaFrambois's bones, something moved. A single item remained where the bones once rested.

Emma's flashlight. It sat upright, still flickering weakly—until it suddenly flared bright white, then died completely.

Emma slept soundly in her room, her breath slow, peaceful. On her nightstand sat her tea cup, still stained with dried lavender.

But inside her mirror, her reflection did not sleep.

It smiled—not because it was happy, but because it was finally close enough to touch her.

BULLSEYE

JASON Price hated clowns.

Not in the silly "ugh, they're weird" kind of way. Jason hated clowns the way some kids hated homework, or chores, or bee stings. Their white makeup war paint with a big nose and a smile too wide and fake made his stomach twist. Jason hated clowns. Period.

So when Jason's mom surprised him with tickets to the Baldoni Brothers Traveling Circus coming to Detroit to raise money for the Detroit Public Schools Homework Helpers Fund, he smiled and said "Cool," and immediately decided he'd bring his slingshot. Just in case.

The circus covered a good portion of Campus Martius with neon banners and crooked metal fences. Rusted carnival rides spun in lazy circles while their carnie operators collected tickets and explained rules. Inside the big top, families packed onto wooden benches. Sticky popcorn clung to the floor like flypaper.

Jason sat next to his mom, who was loving every second. "Isn't this fun?" she said, clapping as jugglers twirled flaming clubs.

"Yeah," Jason lied, gripping the slingshot in his hoodie pocket like a rosary.

Then *he* appeared.

Not center ring. Not introduced.

Just *there*. Standing off to the side near the elephants' enclosure. A clown, but not like the others. This one wore a tattered purple suit with ruffled cuffs and a cracked porcelain mask painted in a permanent, miserable frown. He didn't move. He didn't wave. He just stared right at Jason. Jason held his breath. Just then, the lights dimmed, and the ringmaster shouted, "And now, our aerial finale!"

Spotlights spun. The crowd gasped. Jason took his chance. He pulled a steel marble from his pocket, loaded the slingshot, aimed, pulled back hard as he could, and let go.

The marble struck the clown square in the rear. Jason held his laughter, only to realize in this moment the situation wasn't funny. The clown flinched violently, like a marionette being yanked by unseen strings. His head slowly turned slowly toward Jason. The porcelain mask didn't shift, but something behind the eyeholes did. When their eyes locked, Jason's blood ran cold. Then the circus lights flared, the crowd roared, and the moment passed.

Jason didn't look that way again.

Later that evening, Jason rode his bike home with his best friend Micah. The crescent moon cast long shadows over cracked sidewalks as Jason told Micah what happened.

Jason's and Micah's BMX tires hummed over the asphalt. "You're seriously telling me you *shot* a clown?" Micah asked for the third time.

Jason grinned. "Dead center on the butt cheek. Dude flinched like someone tazed him."

"No way."

"I did the world a favor."

Micah snorted. "You've got issues. I mean, I hate clowns too, but I'm not gonna go full sniper on one."

Jason shrugged. A scowl formed on his face. "They deserve it."

"Okay, but like what if he comes for you?" Micah asked, grinning. "What if he's, like, psycho? And you just signed your death warrant."

Jason laughed. "Bring it on. I got good aim."

They rolled past the corner convenience store. The store loomed dark and silent.

Flop.

Jason slowed his bike. "Did you hear that?"

Micah coasted to a stop. "What?"

Flop. Flop. Flop. Like heavy shoes slapping pavement. Rhythmically—hard heel to heavy toe.

"Weird," Micah said.

Jason looked back. No one. Still, he could *feel* something behind him. Something just out of sight. They pedaled faster.

Flop. Flop. Flop.

Micah hissed, "Okay, *now* I hear it."

Jason's pulse roared in his ears. "Let's move."

They picked up speed. Trees blurred past. Every time they passed a streetlight, shadows shifted unnaturally behind them.

"Jason," Micah cried, "he's following us."

Jason risked a glance back. A tall figure in a purple suit stood under the flickering streetlight, its cracked mask tilted toward them. The eyes, two black holes, stared straight into him. "Oh no," Jason breathed. "No, no, no."

He pumped his legs. Hard.

They skid into Jason's driveway.

Jason flung his bike down, heart slamming against his ribs. "Inside. Now."

Micah bolted after him. They slammed the front door shut, locking it.

Jason flicked on the kitchen light. Empty.

Micah wheezed, hands on his knees. "Dude, what the hell. What *was* that thing?"

Jason shook his head. "It was the clown. It's *him*. I hit him, and now he's . . ." He trailed off.

Micah followed his gaze to the kitchen

counter. A red foam nose sat there. Neither of them moved.

Jason muttered, "That wasn't here before."

From down the hallway came the unmistakable sound: *Squeeeeak. Flop. Flop.*

A shadow passed across the hallway nightlight.

Jason and Micah backed away.

From the shadows, the clown emerged. No mask. Its face was pale, skin stretched tight like rubber. Its grin gaped like a broken jack-o'-lantern, crammed full of tiny, yellow teeth, and its eyes were shark-like, devoid of compassion.

It spoke, not with a voice, but a gravelly and choking laugh. "Bullseye . . . bozo."

Jason screamed.

Micah turned to run. The lights blew out with a crack and the room plunged into darkness.

Jason's skin chilled as something enormous stepped forward.

The next morning, Jason's mom found him asleep on the kitchen floor. Micah was gone. There was no sign of forced entry, just one thing out of place: a single steel marble sat on the counter, blood smeared.

Jason wouldn't speak for days.

People whispered that Micah probably ran away. That boys play rough, take dares, go too far. Jason never corrected them.

But sometimes, on quiet nights, when the wind moves just right and shadows pool at the end of the driveway, Jason hears it:

Flop. Flop. Squeak.

WENDIGO

IN winter, after the tourists left and the fudge shops closed, Mackinac Island became a different place—quiet, icy, almost forgotten.

The Gladieux family came from a long line of islanders. Having owned and operated the island's only market for over a century, they'd heard countless tales from the Ojibwe elders, especially about the wendigo—the eater of flesh, the winter devil that comes when the snow falls hard and deep. But these days, they were modern people. They had Wi-Fi, snowmobiles, and an air fryer. Wendigos weren't nearly as frightening as power blackouts.

Old Leonard Kwadin adjusted his coyote fur shawl as he stood in the canned vegetable aisle at Gladieux's Market, warning Caleb and Josie Gladieux about the beast. They smiled politely, exchanging short glances with each other the entire time.

"The first snow's a curse this year," Kwadin said, looking slowly around the store before locking eyes with Caleb. "The island's due."

Caleb Gladieux was sixteen, and in his mind, only children believed in curses. His sister Josie, two years younger, stayed close behind him, visibly nervous after old Kwadin's ominous warning. Caleb cocked his head and stared at Kwadin. "Due for what?"

Leonard Kwadin gazed at Caleb. "You young people think you know it all," he said, his lips tight, revealing darkened gums and yellow-stained teeth. He pointed his finger at Caleb. "For the hunger. For him. He's out there, and he's gonna get someone. He always comes in storms like these."

Caleb smirked. "Right. Looks like you better get home then and fire up the snow blower."

Kwadin's eyes thinned, and he stared at Caleb a moment too long. He shook his head and walked away, adjusting his coyote shawl, leaving a few strands of hair fall in his wake.

Josie tapped Caleb's arm. "You believe him?"

Caleb scoffed, "He's an idiot."

That night, a storm hit the island, wind howling over the rooftops like a freight train.

Just before midnight, as Caleb lay in his bed listening to music, the house shook with a violent gust. The power went out. Caleb sighed, turned to his side, and closed his eyes.

The storm did not rest. The next day, and the day after, the snow continued to pile up. The island was on its own. The ferry stopped. Help would not be coming.

And something else arrived with the snow. It began with scratching.

Outside the kitchen window, just beyond the beam of their flashlight, they heard it. A disturbing scraping on the siding, like finger-nails on a chalkboard.

"Probably a branch," muttered their father, Peter, as he secured plywood over the window.

But Caleb, watching from the stairwell,

knew something was wrong. There were no trees on that side of the house.

The scratching sound moved. First to the front porch, then the attic vents, even the cellar door. It circled the house all night.

The next morning, they found weird tracks in the snow—long, deep gouges, far too big for a dog or a deer. They almost looked human, except for the backward-turned feet and claw marks.

"I'm telling you, it's just a prank," said Peter, though his voice wavered.

But Nana Gladieux, who hadn't spoken much since the winter her husband died, stirred in her recliner. "You're wrong," she whispered. "You laughed at the old stories. Now it's come to see what's funny. We're going to pay," she said with chilling certainty.

Without a sound, a cry, a scream, *anything*, Nana disappeared that night. No broken window and no footprints leading away, just a trail of dark droplets melting into the snow. And claw marks on the ceiling above her bed.

Josie and Caleb stared at the ceiling, at

the marks. "She warned us," Josie whispered, her voice trembling. "She warned us."

Caleb couldn't answer. He couldn't even move.

They tried to call for help on the CB radio, but it was dead. Worse, the generator wouldn't turn over. It wasn't long before the candles burned low. Outside, the storm screamed ever louder, and the *thing* came closer.

Caleb was the first to see it, standing on the ridge above the house. It had antlers like trees struck by lightning, jagged and broken. Its mouth was huge, gaping, and its large, round eyes were clearly visible even in the raging blizzard. It moved strangely, like a marionette—jerky, yet intentional. It watched the house for hours, waiting for something, taunting the family from the cold darkness.

Finally, Peter felt he had to take matters into his own hands. He grabbed his hunting rifle from its place atop the mantle and went out after it. Minutes ticked past, the family waiting, watching, listening for anything.

The gun was never fired. Peter Gladieux never came back.

Eventually, Caleb ran out to search for him, ignoring his mother's pleas for him to stay. He found one of his father's boots, still warm, and his blood-stained wedding ring too. Nothing else was left of his father. Caleb blamed himself for not going outside with Peter, and punched a hole in the wall in anger. He cried himself to sleep. His mother disappeared that night, swallowed by the storm.

By the third night, it was just Caleb and Josie, huddled by the fireplace with only an axe and Nana's old rosary.

"Don't look at its eyes," Josie whispered.

"Why?"

"Nana said if you do, it knows you see it. And then it gets in."

Caleb didn't listen.

After days of violent wind and relentless snow, all sound and movement came to a stop. For some reason, the stillness was even worse than the storm. Caleb and Josie held each other, waiting.

That's when the thing came to the window. It pressed itself against the glass, grinning, hungry. With a disgusting sound, its jaw unhinged, wider than any human's, it was full of yellow, rotted teeth. It didn't fog the glass. It didn't even breathe. It broke the glass and started to climb in.

"Run!" Caleb shrieked.

They plunged into the snow, boots kicking up powder as the cold seized their lungs with every breath. Behind them, the thing climbed back out of the window and did not chase.

It waited.

Josie's breath came in ragged bursts. "It's not following," she gasped.

"That's what it wants," Caleb said, not turning around. "It wants us to stop."

The island was a maze of snowdrifts and silence. Somewhere far behind them, a door slammed.

Fort Mackinac loomed ahead like a ghost from another century, its white walls blending into the landscape. They shoved open the creaking side door and stumbled inside, boots skidding on the old floorboards.

It was cold inside, colder than it should've been. Puffs of vapor pulsed from Josie and Caleb's mouths as they moved toward the glow and warmth of radiant sunlight slanting through the only window.

Caleb barred the door with an iron rod from an old cannon display. Josie collapsed near the window. "We'll wait here," she said. "Sun's out. Maybe it doesn't like the light?"

Caleb didn't answer. He was listening. The wind? No . . . breathing. Too slow, too deep, too wet.

Josie wiped her eyes and a noise caused her to look to the corner of the room. Nothing. "I think—" she started.

The floorboards creaked. Then, the rafters. The walls. The entire building.

Caleb turned, slow as ice melting.

It was already inside. Antlers scraped the ceiling. Its long arms stretched unnaturally to drag across the walls, its claws carving into the stone and wood. It had no smell. No heat. Just presence.

Josie screamed as it grabbed her. The claws pierced without blood at first, then it came, a dark red ribbon across the old floor.

"Let her go!" Caleb swung the axe. But he hit nothing. Only cold air and darkness followed by an awful cracking and sinister laughter.

"Josie!" he sobbed, over and over, until he couldn't.

By morning there was nothing left except blood-stained snow and drag marks leading into the trees—and a few strands of coyote hair.

*Hey! If you liked these stories,
leave a review on Amazon. Thanks!*

JIM Bolone was born and raised in Detroit, Michigan, and holds a B.A. in English from Wayne State University. His life path has included work as a bartender, waiter, historical interpreter, and drummer. He has shared his passion for storytelling as a junior high creative writing teacher in Ohio. A dedicated writer, Jim has published numerous short stories and is the co-author of three best-selling novels.